Creative Writing, Drawing & Doodling

Purposeful Desk-Work Activities That Improve Literacy, Develop Thinking Skills, and Inspire Creativity

**Written and Illustrated by
Julie Anderson**

Key Education
An imprint of Carson-Dellosa Publishing, LLC
Greensboro, North Carolina

keyeducationpublishing.com

CONGRATULATIONS ON YOUR PURCHASE OF A KEY EDUCATION PRODUCT!

The editors at Key Education are former teachers who bring experience, enthusiasm, and quality to each and every product. Thousands of teachers have looked to the staff at Key Education for new and innovative resources to make their work more enjoyable and rewarding. Key Education is committed to developing and publishing educational materials that will assist teachers in building a strong and developmentally appropriate curriculum for young children.

PLAN FOR GREAT TEACHING EXPERIENCES WHEN YOU USE EDUCATIONAL MATERIALS FROM KEY EDUCATION PUBLISHING

Credits

Author: Julie Anderson
Illustrations: Julie Anderson
Editor: Claude Chalk
Production: Key Education Production Staff
Cover Photograph: © Shutterstock

Dedication

This book is dedicated to my creative writing, drawing, and doodling son, Tate. He adds an abundant amount of laughter and craziness to our lives and has an imagination that will take the world by storm someday! We love you, Shmoo!

Key Education
An imprint of Carson-Dellosa Publishing, LLC
PO Box 35665
Greensboro, NC 27425 USA
carsondellosa.com

ISBN 1-978-162057-365-5
01-002138091

Introduction

Do you have a daydreamer you need to teach, whether it be in the classroom or at home? How about a child who doodles on every paper she can get her hands on? Or, a student who struggles with learning but loves to write and draw pictures?

I am a parent of a child who fits all of these descriptions. He struggles with focus and math concepts. He is also a terrific writer. His head is always in the clouds, and his schoolwork is decorated with superheroes. That is why I created this book. This book is for children with vivid imaginations and for those who need a little creative inspiration. It is meant to encourage creativity in the classroom, as well as in everyday life.

This book can be used in different ways. It could be used in the middle of the day to give tired or bored minds a burst of creativity. It could be enjoyed in place of an art class that has been cut because of a tight school budget. It could also be given as a reward to a distractible child who finished his schoolwork.

Just as each child has a different learning style, this book includes different activities to challenge each child's creative side. For children who love to write, there are stories to finish and a lot of space for their minds to go to work. For those who love to draw, there is plenty of room for imaginations to run wild. For doodlers, there are pages with lines and squiggles to get them started. What each finished picture will be depends on how each child sees it. Whether for a child who is a creative thinker or one who struggles to find the right word or picture, this book provides endless possibilities for creative learning.

Table of Contents

Unbelievable Catch!

Directions: Draw what you think he caught.

Name _____

Me & My Friend

Directions: On the lines below, write five things that you like about a friend.
Then, draw a picture of you and your friend doing something that you both like to do.

1. _____

2. _____

3. _____

4. _____

5. _____

 Me & _____

Name _____

If You Were An Animal . . .

Directions: Draw what kind of animal you would like to be.

The Day I Got a New _____

Directions: Read the story and fill in the blanks. Then, draw a picture of your finished story.

I always dreamed of having my own _____.

My dad finally decided that because I was _____,

I was ready! My dad and I drove to the _____.

We looked at all of the _____. Then, I saw it!

I knew right away that it was the right one for me!

My dad smiled. I laughed. It was the _____

day ever!

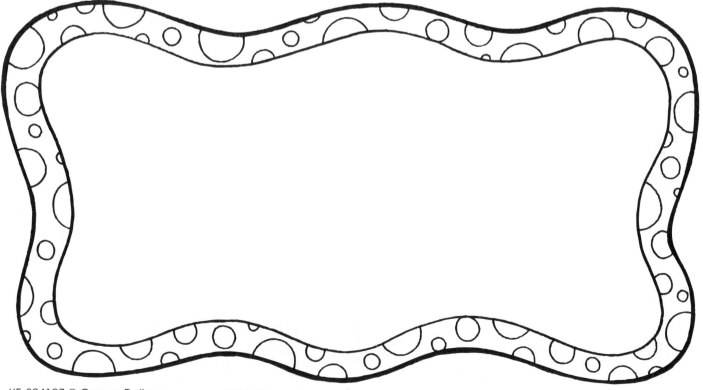

Creative Writing, Drawing & Doodling

An Amazing Discovery

Directions: You just made an amazing discovery!
Draw a picture of what you found on the leaf.

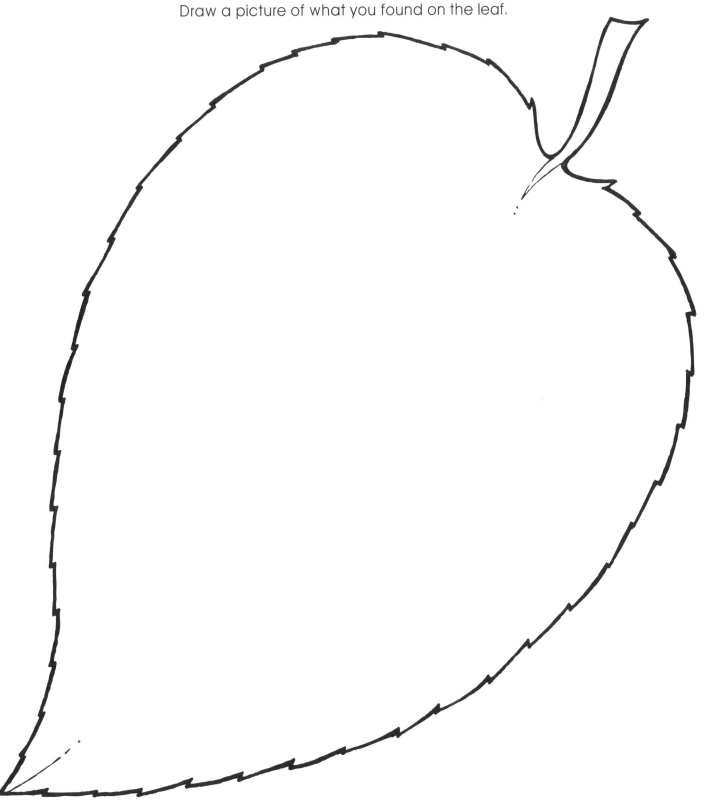

Name _____

Who Is Your Hero?

Directions: Write a paragraph about your hero. Then, draw a picture of you and your hero.

- 10 -

Be a Clown

Directions: The circus just asked you to be a clown. Design your clown costume.

Doodle 1

Directions: Finish the doodle.

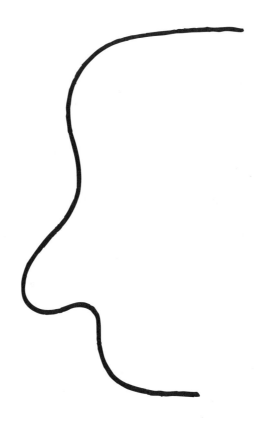

Magic Tricks!

Directions: Pretend that you are a magician.

Draw a few things in the box that you might need to use in your magic show.

A New Planet

Directions: You discovered a new planet.
Name your planet and draw "who" or "what" lives there.

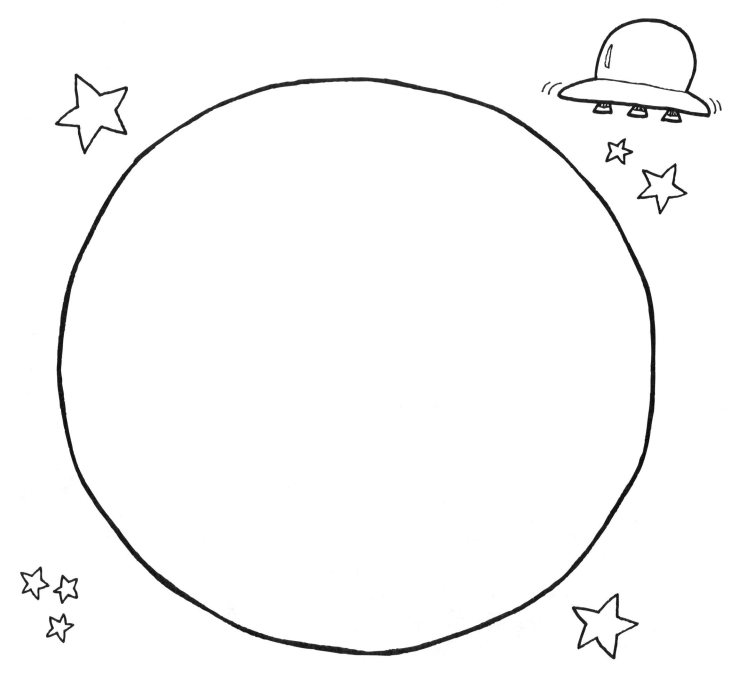

PLANET _____

Bake Sale!

Directions: Decorate the cookies for your school's bake sale.

Creative Writing, Drawing & Doodling

I Am a Superhero!

Directions: Draw yourself as a new superhero that the world has not yet seen!
Give yourself a name.

The Amazing _____

Name _____

My Superhero Adventure

Directions: Write a story about yourself as an amazing superhero.

Doodle 2

Directions: Finish the doodle.

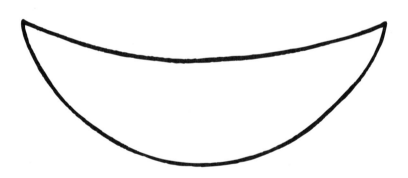

   - 18 -   **Creative Writing, Drawing & Doodling**

Name _____

The Bear and the Fish

Directions: Write what you think the bear and the fish are saying to each other.

Creative Writing, Drawing & Doodling

My Family

Directions: Draw and color a picture of your family.

My Best Gift Ever!

Directions: Draw a picture of the best gift that you have ever received.
Then, write why this gift was so special to you.

_____

- -

_____

- -

_____

Doodle 3

Directions: Finish the doodle.

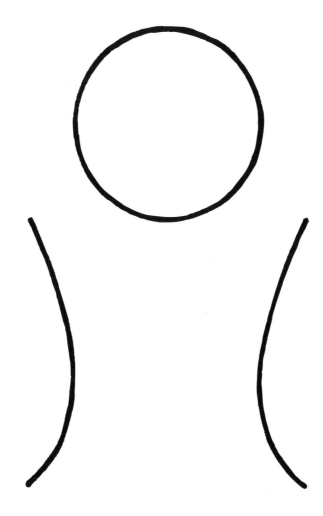

Dreaming Dragon

Directions: Write about what you think the dragon is dreaming.
Then, draw a picture of the dragon's dream. Be careful not to wake him up!

Name _____

What Are You Thinking?

Directions: Draw whatever is in your head!

Name _____

All Grown Up

Directions: What do you want to be when you grow up? Write about it and then draw a picture.

I want to be a _____

because _____

Doodle 4

Directions: Finish the doodle.

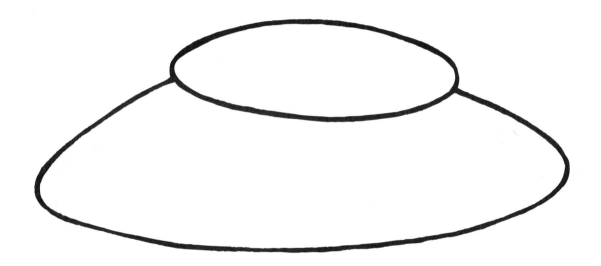

What a Tree!

Directions: Name and draw a picture of what is growing on the tree.

Have you ever seen a tree that grows _____?

Name _____

Really Good!

Directions: Read and then write your answers.

Write about something you are really good at.

_____
_____
_____
_____
_____
_____
_____
_____

Write about something that you would like to be good at.

_____
_____
_____
_____
_____
_____

Name _____

Team Family

Directions: You are going to a family reunion. Design a T-shirt for your family to wear.

Ahoy, Mate!

Directions: Turn yourself into a swashbuckling pirate! Don't forget the parrot!

The Pirate Captain

Directions: Pretend that you are the pirate captain. You are hunting for buried treasure. Write about your adventure. What treasure did you find?

_____

- -

_____

- -

_____

- -

_____

- -

_____

- -

_____

- -

_____

- -

_____

- -

_____

- -

_____

- -

_____

- -

_____

- -

- -

Finish the Face

Directions: Draw a happy, sad, or silly face. Draw any face you want!

Comic Strip

Directions: Write what you think the characters are saying to each other. Color the pictures.

Name _____

KE-804107 © Carson-Dellosa

Creative Writing, Drawing & Doodling

Name _____

I Baked a Cake!

Directions: You just baked a wonderful cake. Draw a picture of your cake on the plate.
Then, write the recipe on the card below.

Recipe for my famous _____ **cake**

_____

_____

_____

_____

_____

_____

_____

Car of the Future

Directions: Design a car of the future.
Then, write about all of the special things that your car can do.

_____

_____

_____

_____

_____

_____

Doodle 5

Directions: Finish the doodle.

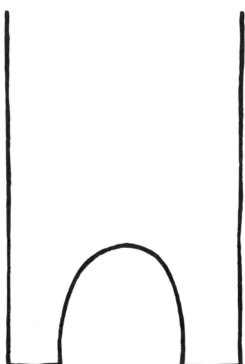

I'm Going to the Ball!

Directions: Design a beautiful ball gown and hairdo (fit for a princess)
or royal clothes (fit for a prince) that you can wear to the royal ball. Be sure to add a crown!

Name _____

If I Could . . .

Directions: Finish the story and then draw a picture of it.

If I could do anything, I would

_____

_ _

_____

_ _

_____

_ _

_____

_ _

_____

Name _____

I  U

Directions: Write a letter to your mom, dad, or grandparents and tell them why they are special to you.

Doodle 6

Directions: Finish the doodle.

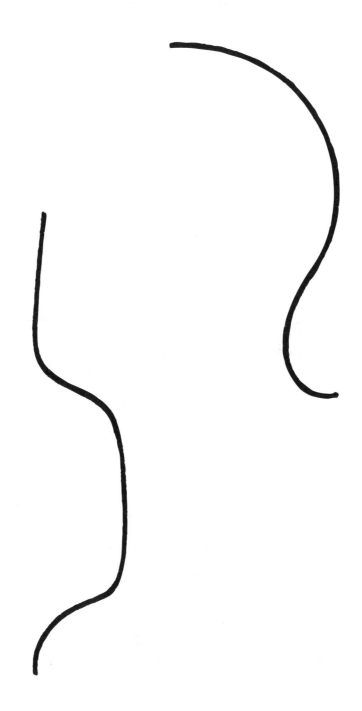

What a Hat!

Directions: Design a hat. Make it fun and silly.

Speak Up!

Directions: Write in the speech bubbles what you think the lady and the frog are saying to each other.

The Seasons

Directions: Draw a picture of you playing in each season.

spring	summer
autumn	winter

Close Your Eyes

Directions: Draw something with your eyes closed.

Name _____

Mystery of the Missing _____

Directions: Finish the story by filling in the blanks. Then, draw a picture of what was missing.

Last night, I left some _____ on the table. When I woke up, it was missing!

"Mom, have you seen my _____?" I asked.

Mom said, "I saw it in the _____ with Dad."

"Dad, have you seen my _____?" I asked.

"I did," said Dad, "but your sister needed it for her _____."

"Sis, have you seen my _____?" I asked.

"Yes," she said, "but, I put it back on the table."

Then, all of a sudden, my _____ ran by. It was all over him!

"Mystery solved!" chuckled Dad.

Creative Writing, Drawing & Doodling

Doodle 7

Directions: Finish the doodle.

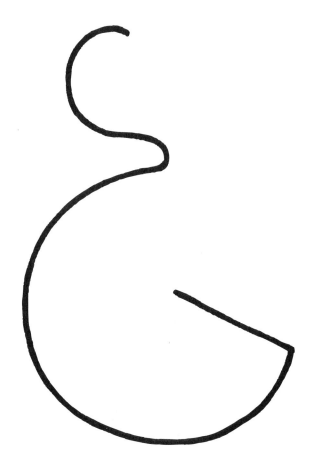

Animal Antics

Directions: Look at the shapes in the grass. Turn the shapes into bugs or animals.

My Favorite Foods

Directions: Write a list of your favorite foods. Then, draw and color those foods.

My Favorite Foods

1. _____
2. _____
3. _____
4. _____
5. _____
6. _____

Ice Cream Fun

Directions: Create your own ice-cream cone. What are your favorite flavors?
Can you invent some new flavors?

Teacher's New Do

Directions: Draw and color your teacher with a new hairstyle.

Creative Writing, Drawing & Doodling

Two-Handed Drawing

Directions: Tape this paper to your desk. Hold two pencils, one in each hand.
Now, at the same time, finish drawing this face. Can you draw with both hands at the same time?
When you are done, do you think that both sides look the same?

Name _____

Under the Stars – part 1

Directions: Finish the story by filling in the blanks with words or pictures.

Last summer, my family went on a camping trip. We packed the cars

with _____, _____, and _____.

As we drove, we saw a lot of _____. My brother and I were

very excited.   Our campsite was our favorite place to go because it is in

the _____.   We finally arrived and got the campsite ready.

My dad and I set up the _____.   My brother and mom set out

to look for _____.   After that, we built a _____ and

got ready to cook.   We made _____, _____, and

_____.   It was the best food we had ever eaten.

Next, we went on a hike. We saw a rare _____. Then, my

dad got chased by a _____. We laughed because it was only

a _____.

The sun went down, and it was time to _____. We climbed

into our _____. Suddenly, we heard a _____

and saw a shadow.   My brother screamed, but I saw it. It was only a

_____. We laughed and looked at all of the _____

in the sky. But, we did not want to go back to _____.

Name _____

Under the Stars – part 2

Directions: Draw a picture to go with your story "Under the Stars — part 1."

Doodle 8

Directions: Finish the doodle.

I Am a Famous Inventor!

Directions: Draw a picture of your latest and greatest invention.
Write about what your invention can do.

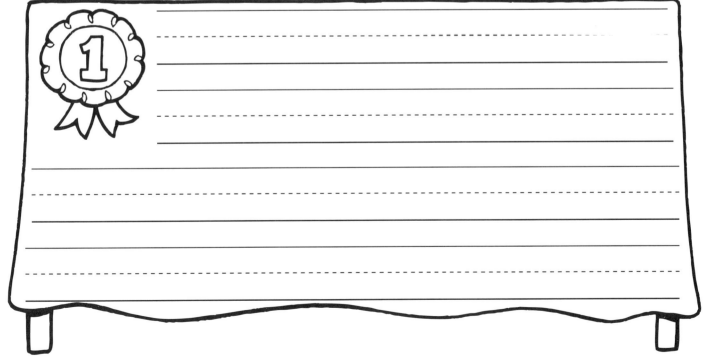

On the Road

Directions: Draw your favorite place at the end of the road.

5 MILES

Name _____

I Need a Disguise!

Directions: You are trying to hide from your sister. Draw and color a disguise. Be creative. Make sure she will not recognize you.

Name _____

My Favorite Pizza

Directions: Write a list of your favorite pizza toppings. Then, draw and color your pizza.
Be creative. Make any kind of pizza you would like.

Pizza Toppings

1. _____

2. _____

3. _____

4. _____

5. _____

6. _____

7. _____

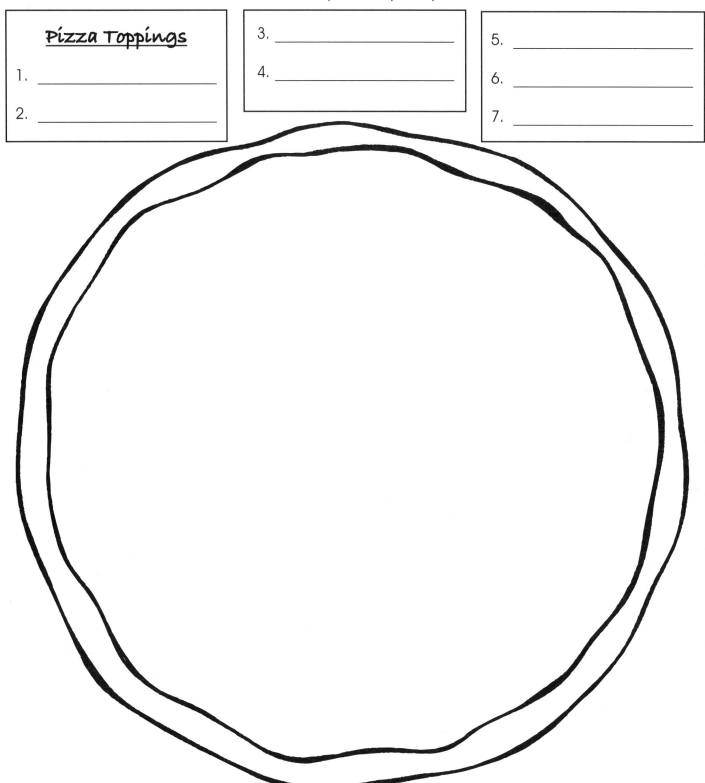

Name _____

What a School!

Directions: Write a story to go with this picture.

_____
- -
_____
- -
_____
- -
_____
- -
_____
- -
_____
- -
_____
- -
_____
- -
_____

Doodle 9

Directions: Finish the doodle.

What Do You See?

Directions: Look at the clouds. What do you see in the clouds?
Finish by drawing pictures in the clouds. Then, write about what you see.

Name _____

The Perfect Food – part 1

Directions: Fill in the blanks with words or pictures.

Recipe for the perfect _____

Ingredients:

1 cup _____

1/2 cup _____

3 small _____

2 large _____

1 tablespoon _____

1 teaspoon _____

A dash of _____

grated _____

Directions:

In a large _____, mix the _____, _____, and _____. In a small _____, whisk together the _____ and _____. Sprinkle a little _____ and _____ and stir with a _____.

Next, pour the _____ into the _____.

Finally, pour into a _____ and bake for _____ minutes at _____ degrees. Serve with some _____.